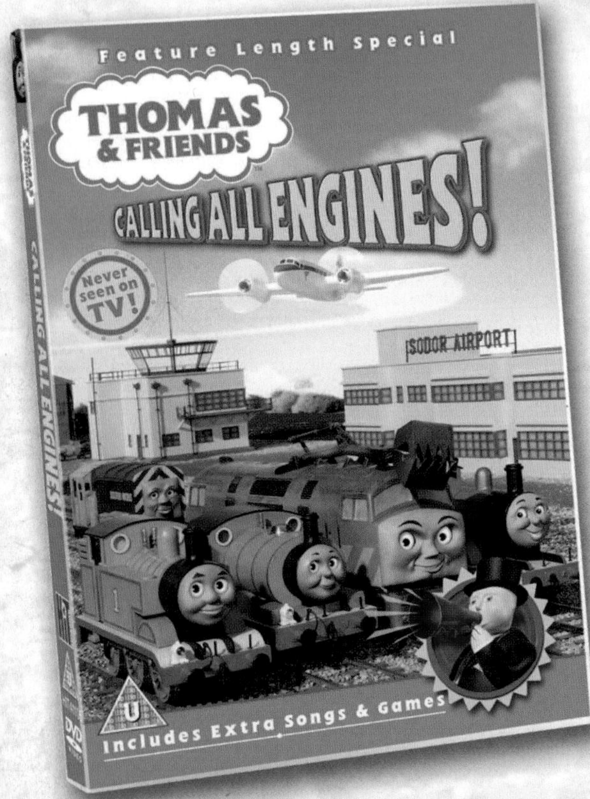

CALLING ALL ENGINES!

is the first ever direct to DVD special
for Thomas and friends.
When Sir Topham Hatt announces the building
of a new airport on Sodor, old rivalries between
steam engines and diesels soon resurface.
A trick by Thomas backfires badly and before
long the whole plan is on the brink of collapse.
Can Thomas persuade the diesel and steam
engines to settle their differences and get the
island back on track?

**Calling All Engines! DVD is available
to own in Autumn 2005**

For further information go to www.thomasandfriends.com

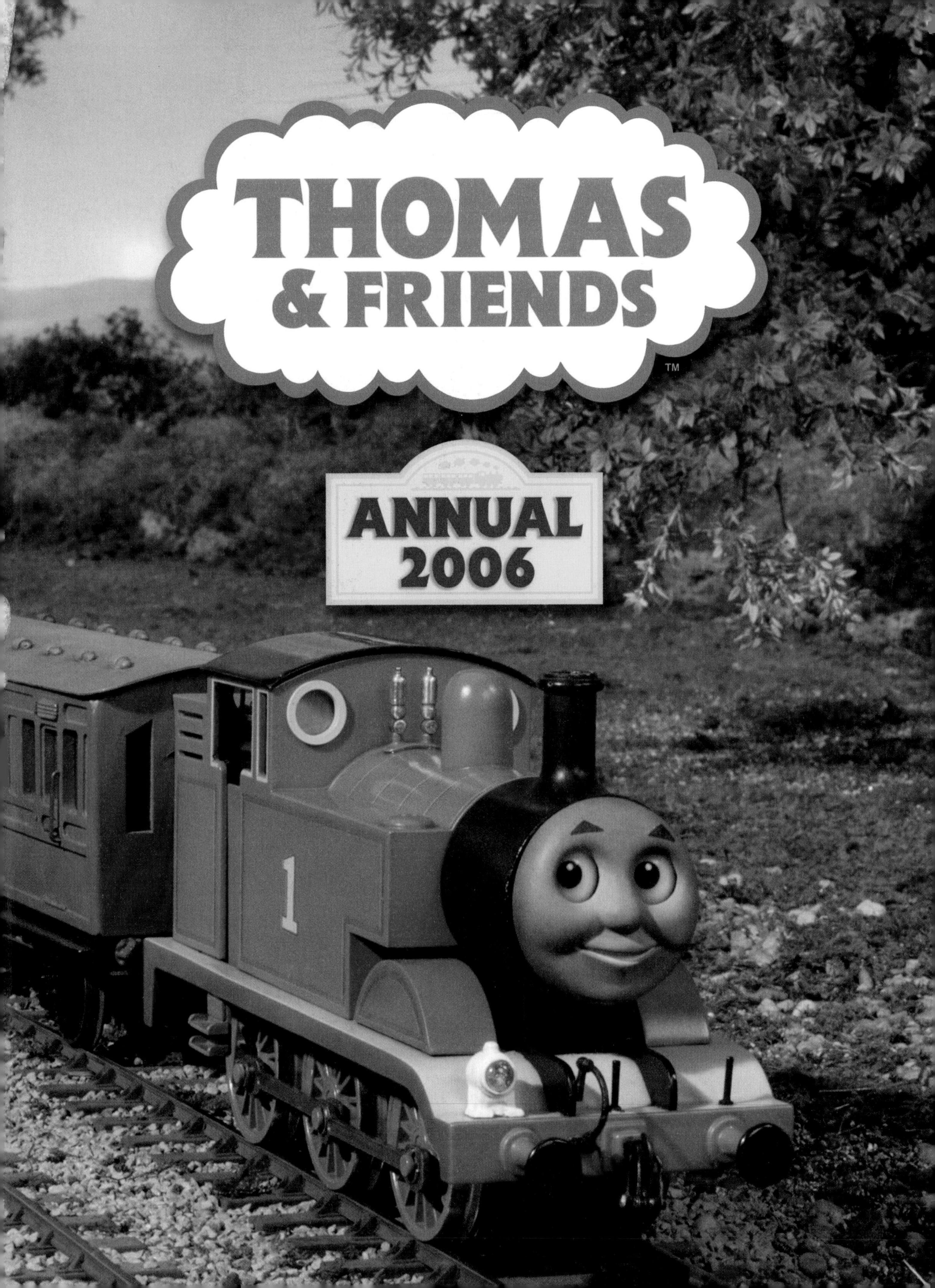
THOMAS
& FRIENDS
TM
ANNUAL
2006
1

Contents

EGMONT
We bring stories to life
Published in Great Britain 2005 by Egmont Books Limited,
239 Kensington High Street, London W8 6SA

Printed in Italy
ISBN 1 4052 2105 4
10 9 8 7 6 5 4 3 2 1

Thomas the Tank Engine & Friends
A BRITT ALLCROFT COMPANY PRODUCTION
Based on The Railway Series by The Rev W Awdry

Hello and welcome to my new annual!

I hope you'll enjoy reading about me and my engine friends. We all like to work hard – especially me! – but we like to have fun, too. You can read stories about Percy and a magic carpet, the day I brought the circus to town, Emily and the Black Loch Monster – and lots more!

Have fun!

Your friend,

THOMAS

Meet Thomas and his friends

"**Peep!** My name is **Thomas**, and I'm a tank engine. I may be little, but I work very hard and I always try to be on time. That's why I'm the Really Useful Number 1 engine! I'm very proud to have my very own branch line that takes workmen to and from the Quarry."

"My name is **Sir Topham Hatt**, but everyone calls me The Fat Controller. I'm in charge of the railway on the Island of Sodor. It's my job to make sure the engines all do their jobs properly, so that the passengers are never late."

"I'm **Annie** and I'm one of Thomas' coaches. I'm quite old and made of wood, but I can still work hard all day. I carry passengers and I always travel facing Thomas."

"I'm **Clarabel**, Thomas' other coach, and I've got two sections. The passengers travel in one and the other is for the Guard and luggage. I travel behind Annie, facing away from Thomas."

"I'm **Trevor** and I'm a traction engine. I run on roads instead of rails and I live in a shed at the bottom of the orchard at the Vicarage. I love taking children for rides."

"Hello there! I'm **Percy**, the Number 6 engine, and I'm always happy to puff around the yard with the trucks. I love playing tricks on Thomas. He doesn't mind because he's my very special friend!"

"I'm the blue Number 2 engine and my name is **Edward**. I'm a bit older than the other engines and I try to be kind to them all, no matter how cheeky they are. I'm even kind to the trucks!"

"My name is **Henry** and I'm the green Number 3 engine. I'm a very high class engine, and I'm proud to be very long, very fast – and very strong."

"I'm the fastest and most powerful of The Fat Controller's engines and I'm sure you know my name. Yes, I'm **Gordon** the big blue Number 4 Express engine."

"Hello, I'm **James**, and I'm the medium-sized Number 5 engine – smaller than Gordon, but bigger than Thomas! My bright red paint and shiny brass dome make me a Really Splendid Engine."

"My name is **Harold**, though Thomas sometimes calls me Whirlybird, because I'm a helicopter. I don't have to run on rails, like the engines – I can fly anywhere I like."

"I'm **Toby**, Number 7, and I'm a tram engine. Some people say I'm old fashioned but I still do very Useful work on the Quarry line. My coach is called Henrietta."

"I'm **Bertie** the single-decker red bus, and I'm one of Thomas' best friends. The engines think they are very Useful, but I am, too, and I'm always happy to help them!"

"Hello there, mateys! **Salty**'s my name and I work at Brendam Docks where I shunt the trains in place behind the engines. I like my work – and I love telling stories."

"I'm **Cranky the Crane** and I work at the Docks, too. I'm very Useful because I can load and unload all sorts of things from the ships and trains."

"My name is **Emily**. I haven't been on the Island for long, but I like it here because The Fat Controller has lots of jobs for me to do. I always try to be kind to the others."

"My name is **Murdoch** and I'm a very strong engine – strong enough to pull the longest goods trains. My paint is an unusual colour. Some people say it's yellow, but I know it's gold!"

"I'm **Diesel** and I'm a shunting engine. I like to cause trouble in the engine sheds whenever I can, which is why the other engines call me Devious Diesel. But I don't care – I **like** being sneaky!"

Thomas and the circus

The engines were very excited because the circus was coming to town!

Percy wanted to see the dancing horses.

James couldn't wait to see the funny clowns.

And Thomas? He just wanted to see the big-top tent go up!

All the engines wanted to be the one to go to the Docks to collect the circus, but who would The Fat Controller choose?

It was Thomas!

"But Thomas, if there are too many trucks for you to pull you must share the work with the other engines," said The Fat Controller.

"Yes, Sir, I will," said Thomas, and he steamed off with Annie and Clarabel.

At the Docks, Cranky the Crane had unloaded everything. There were horse boxes and costumes and people everywhere.

The acrobats and clowns climbed aboard Annie, and Clarabel carried the ringmaster and the band.

Salty shunted the very long, very heavy circus train into place behind Thomas.

"Need any help, matey?" he asked.

Thomas remembered what The Fat Controller had said about sharing the work but he wanted to pull the circus train all by himself. "No, thank you, Salty," he said. **"I can do it!"**

Then Thomas took the biggest puff he could and slowly **chuff-chuffed** out into the countryside.

He had to work very hard indeed.

His pistons pumped ...

His traction rods rattled ...

But Thomas was so happy that he took no notice. **"Peep!"**

When Thomas pulled the circus train through Maron Station he got a lovely surprise. The platforms were full of people waving and cheering!

The circus people waved back, and the band played. Thomas was so happy that he joined in by blowing his whistle: **"Peep, peep!"**

When Thomas had to stop at the junction, children lined the bridge to wave and cheer.

"PEEP!" Thomas blew his whistle extra loudly for them.

Percy was there, too. He **REALLY** wanted to help. "Is there anything I can take for you, Thomas?" he asked.

But Thomas wanted to do everything himself. He was having too much fun to accept help from Percy.

"No thank you, Percy," he said. **"I'll do it on my own."**

"Oh, I see," said Percy sadly. He felt very disappointed as he watched Thomas chuff away.

Thomas puffed on ... and on ... and on.

The train felt heavier ... and heavier ... and heavier.

His traction rods rattled ... and rattled ... and rattled!

When he stopped at a signal James was waiting in the siding. Like Percy, he wanted to help with the circus train.

"If you uncouple some trucks I can take them for you," he said.

But Thomas still didn't want any help, even though he was very tired.

"No thank you, James," he said. **"I can do it on my own."**

Thomas steamed off again, but every **huff** was harder, and every **chuff** made him feel more and more tired.

When Thomas passed through the next station he didn't have enough steam to whistle to the people waving from the platform. He couldn't manage even one single tiny toot. He was almost out of puff.

Then out in the countryside – **creak! crack!** – Thomas' traction rods broke, and he stopped with a jolt. **He couldn't move!**

Thomas was worried, and so were the circus people.

"We need to practise," said one of the clowns.

"And the horses need more hay," said the ringmaster.

Thomas' driver telephoned for help and soon James arrived with new traction rods. Percy brought some hay for the horses, too.

"I wanted to keep all the fun to myself," said Thomas. "But now I wish I'd shared the work with you."

"Never mind, we'll **ALL** have fun now!" puffed Percy.

Percy was right!

Thomas got new traction rods, then he shared out the trucks.

Percy took the horses.

James took the performers.

Thomas took the heavy big-top tent.

Then the band started playing and the circus train set off again.

Now, when people waved and cheered, **THREE** engines blew their whistles.

"Peep!" said Thomas. **"This is good fun!"**

Later on, when the circus had been set up, the engines went to look at the big-top tent.

"Peep!" said Thomas. "Thank you for helping me. Sharing work is good because it makes things easier. **But sharing FUN is even better!"**

Spot the difference

There were lots of circus people for Thomas to carry! It was hard work for a little engine!

These two pictures look the same, but there are six things that are different in picture 2. Look very carefully – can you spot them all?

ANSWERS: 1. a funnel is missing; 2. Thomas' whistle is missing; 3. a funnel is a different colour; 4. a clown's outfit is a different colour; 5. one of Thomas' buffers is missing; 6. the end of a coach is a different colour.

"Don't tell Thomas!"

It was cold and the Island of Sodor was covered in a white blanket of snow. But the engines didn't mind at all because it meant that the Christmas holidays would soon be here. And that meant lots of fun!

Thomas loved Christmas time because everyone was happy and jolly. The Stationmasters decorated the stations with twinkling fairy lights and garlands and children made snowmen and sang Christmas songs and carols.

But there was one thing Thomas didn't like about winter – his snowplough. He had to use it so that he could clear the snow from the railway lines but he didn't like it at all.

"Cinders and ashes!" said Thomas. "I need it, so I've just got to put up with it!"

Thanks to all his hard work the lines were kept clear and the trains ran on time. The other engines were very grateful to him.

At Dryan Station, Toby and Harold were planning a surprise for Thomas. It was a thank you for all his hard work.

As Thomas steamed into the station he heard Harold say, "Remember, it's a surprise. **Don't tell Thomas."**

"Don't tell me what?" asked Thomas.

But Harold buzzed up into the air and Toby puffed back to the yard.

Thomas felt cross. He didn't like being left out of things and he **loved** surprises.

That afternoon, Thomas met Percy, whose trucks were full of coloured boxes.

"Are they part of the surprise?" asked Thomas.

But before Percy could reply, Harold hovered over them.

"Sssshhh!" he said.

"Don't tell Thomas!"

Later on, Thomas was puffing along his branch line with his coaches, Annie and Clarabel. He couldn't stop thinking about the surprise. He **REALLY** wanted to know what it was.

He thought about it all the way to the end of the line ...

Then he thought about it all the way back again ...

When Thomas stopped at a signal he saw Emily. She was pulling a long truck with something long and pointy wrapped in a cover.

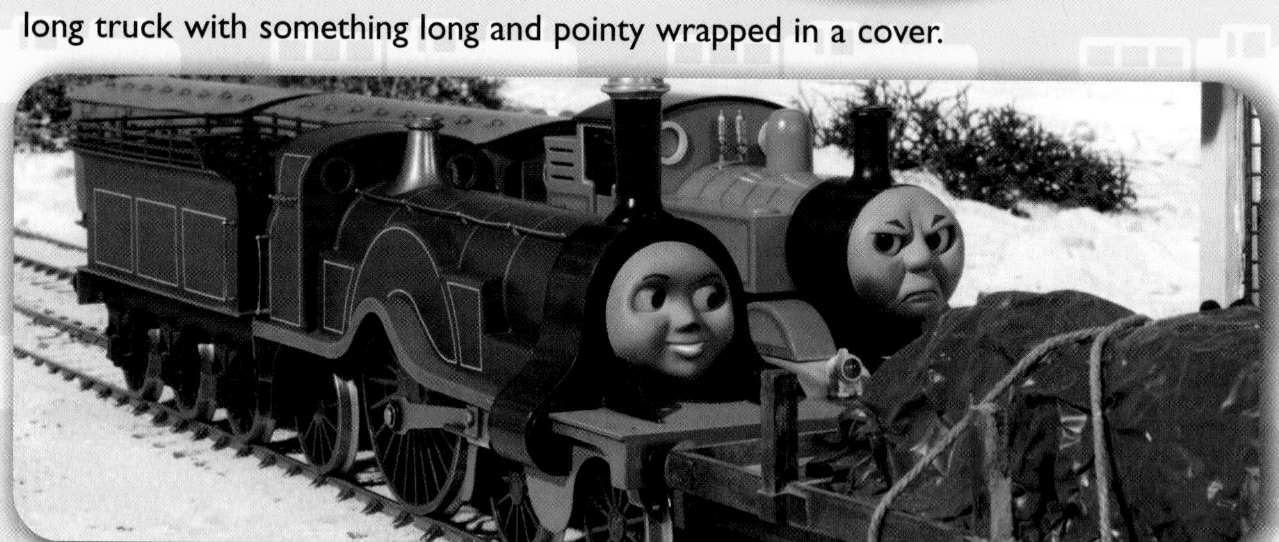

"Is that part of the surprise?" asked Thomas.

"I can't say," said Emily, and she puffed away.

"WHEESH!" said Thomas. "If Emily won't tell me, I'll follow her and find out for myself!"

Thomas puffed along behind Emily as quietly as he could.

He followed her through a tunnel ...

over a bridge ...

past the windmill ...

But when Emily turned on to a branch line, the points changed, and Thomas couldn't follow her.

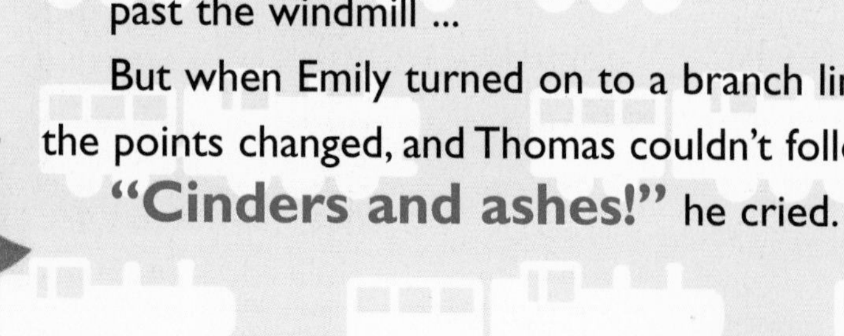

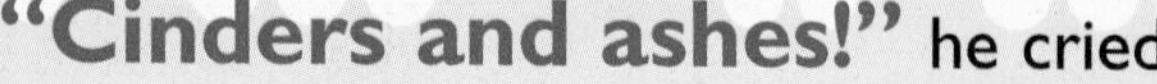

"Cinders and ashes!" he cried.

That night the engines were all talking about the surprise. But they stopped when Thomas chuffed into the sheds.

"Ssssshhh!" said James.

"Don't tell Thomas!" said Henry.

Poor Thomas felt more left out than ever.

"Everyone knows about the surprise except me," he huffed. "Well, if they won't tell me, then **I don't want to know!"**

And with that, Thomas steamed away from the sheds as fast as he could go.

Soon he was far, far away.

When it was time for Thomas' surprise the engines didn't know where he was.

"I'll find him," said Harold.

Thomas was in a siding right on the other side of the Island. He was very cold ... very lonely ... and very sad.

Then he heard a noise above him. It was Harold's whirlybird wings!

"Come on, Thomas!" said Harold. "It's time for you to take the children to see your surprise!"

"My surprise?" said Thomas.

"Yes, it's our way of saying a special thank you for clearing the snow from the lines," said Harold.

"So I wasn't being left out?" said Thomas.

"Of course not!" said Harold. "Now hurry along, old chap, the children are all waiting for you."

Thomas collected the children, then he steamed off past the windmill ... down a branch line ... and into a little village.

That's when Thomas saw his surprise – and what a really lovely surprise it was!

Emily had been carrying a tall Christmas tree! It stood in the village square, shining with twinkly lights and baubles and garlands.

Around the tree were the presents Percy had brought.

Thomas' Driver put shiny tinsel around his funnel – and his **surprise party began!**

"PEEP! This was worth waiting for!" said Thomas. **"It's the best surprise I've ever had!"**

Jigsaw picture fun

Which little jigsaw pieces complete each big picture?

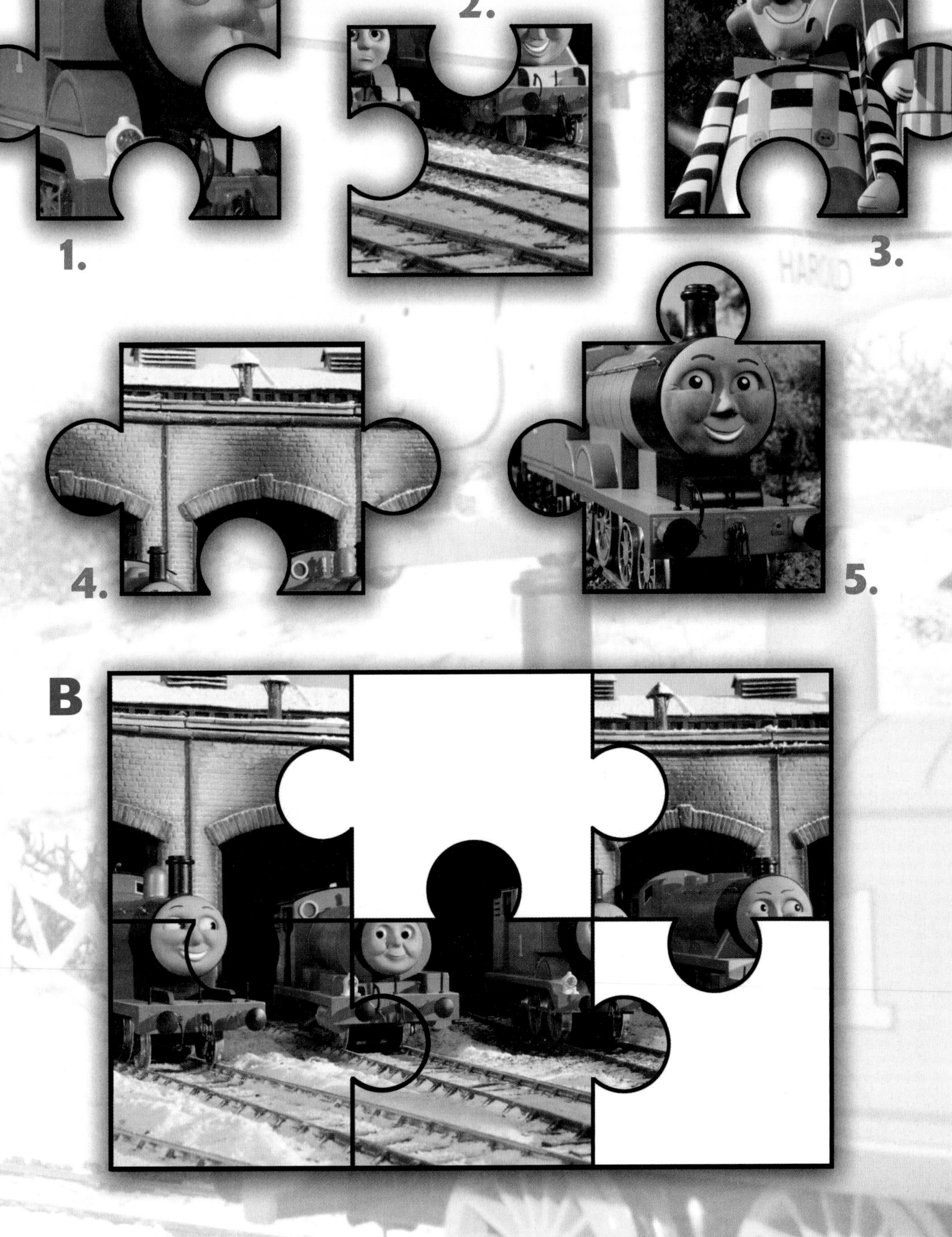

ANSWERS: Jigsaw A, pieces 5 and 3. Jigsaw B, pieces 4 and 2.

A story to colour

Colour in the picture story about Thomas and Gordon as neatly as you can.

Thomas is a cheeky little engine who loves playing tricks.

One day, Gordon was fast asleep after a hard day's work.

Thomas chuffed up and whistled as loudly as he could: **"PEEEEEP!"**

Poor Gordon nearly jumped off the rails!

"Wake up, lazybones!" laughed Thomas. "Get some hard work done for a change!"

"What a cheek!" said Gordon. "I'll show him all about hard work!"

And he did just that.

Thomas always pushed Gordon's train to help him start. He was uncoupled so that he could stop and go back.

But the next morning Gordon started so quickly that there was no time to uncouple Thomas. **Gordon took Thomas with him!**

Gordon went **faster ... and faster ... and faster.**

So did Thomas. **"STOP!"** he whistled.

At last, Gordon stopped. "Now you know all about hard work, don't you, little Thomas?" he said.

Poor Thomas! He was so out of breath that he couldn't answer.

Do you think Thomas learned his lesson?
Can you tell the story in your own words?

Edward the Great

Edward the Number 2 engine has the same blue paintwork as Thomas and is the same size as James.

Edward can pull carriages ... and push trucks ... and he often works as a back engine, pushing the other engines up hills.

But Edward is rather old and he's not quite as strong as he used to be. Because of this, he sometimes feels a bit sad and left out of things.

When the Duke and Duchess of Boxford came to Sodor they travelled on their own train. The engine's name was Spencer and he was big, sleek, silver – and fast, **VERY** fast.

When Spencer pulled into Knapford Station his Driver had some great news for him. "That was a really fast time," he said. "You've beaten Gordon's record."

Spencer let out a **whoosh** of steam. "I'm not surprised," he said. **"I'm faster than all the engines on Sodor put together."**

That made The Fat Controller's engines very cross indeed.

"What a cheek!" said Gordon. "Spencer's just a big silver show-off!"

Spencer was going to take the Duke and Duchess to their holiday house but The Fat Controller needed another engine to take their furniture.

The engines all wanted the job. They wanted to race against Spencer.

"Me, please, Sir!" said Thomas.

"I'll do it!" said James.

"May I go?" said Gordon.

"You all have other important work to do," said The Fat Controller. **"Edward, you can take the furniture."**

"Fancy sending an old back engine to do an Express engine's job," said Gordon.

"He'll lose the race and let us all down," said James.

But Thomas and Percy spoke up for their old friend.

"Spencer is a much bigger engine than Edward," said Thomas. **"But he's full of hot air!"**

"And a good old steamie can beat a pouty puffer any day!" said Percy.

But secretly they weren't sure that Edward really could beat Spencer ...

Edward wobbled out of the station, slow and steady.

"Will-do-my-best, will-do-my-best," he puffed, as Spencer glided past him – **whoosh!** He was **SO** fast and smooth.

Soon Spencer had left Edward far, far behind.

He laughed and said, **"I think I've won the race already!"**

By the time Edward chuffed to the junction at the bottom of Gordon's hill he was out of puff. The furniture was heavy and pulling it was hard work for an old engine. But he huffed and puffed, and got to the top of the hill at last.

Wheeeee! He was much faster going down the other side!

When Spencer stopped for water, Edward caught up with him.

He was still going slow and steady, just as he always did.

"There you are!" said Spencer. "I thought you'd have given up by now."

"Not me!" said Edward crossly as he chuffed past Spencer. "I'm a Sodor engine, and Sodor engines never give up! **NEVER!"**

When Spencer's tank was full he roared past Edward again. "See you when you get there!" he said. **"IF** you ever get there!"

Edward took a deep breath and carried on. **"I-won't-give-up,"** he said. **"I-won't-give-up."**

When Spencer stopped at Crosby Station so that the Duke and Duchess could have tea, Edward caught up with him again.

He wished he could stop for a rest, but the Stationmaster and porters had heard about the race and they cheered him on. **"Hurray for Edward!"** they cried. "He's a fine old Sodor engine!"

That made Edward feel better, so he picked up speed and steamed past Spencer.

But at Dryan Station, Spencer zoomed past Edward again.

"Fastest-and-best," he said. **"Fastest-and-best."**

Poor Edward could only watch as Spencer streaked off into the distance. The furniture felt heavier than ever, and for the first time Edward thought he might have to give up.

But when Spencer stopped so that the Duke could take some photographs, he closed his eyes – and was soon fast asleep!

Gordon thought Spencer was winning the race.

"Edward is a waste of steam!" he hissed.

But when he saw how hard Edward was trying, he felt bad about what he'd said.

"Good work, Edward," he said. "You're trying so hard. You're a credit to the railway, you really are!"

That made Edward feel **MUCH** better and he found some extra puff he didn't know he had.

"I-am-going-to-do-it," he said. **"I-am-going-to-do-it."**

When it was time for Spencer to set off again, his Driver rang his bell. **Ding!** But nothing happened. Spencer was still fast asleep!

He didn't hear the bell – and he didn't hear Edward.

Ding! Ding! Spencer's Driver rang the bell again ... and again ... and again, and at last his eyes opened.

Spencer's eyes opened extra wide when he saw Edward ahead of him, chuffing towards the Duke and Duchess' house!

"Nearly-there," said Edward. **"Nearly-there."**

Spencer set off as fast as he could but he had to slow down on the little branch line. "You're too heavy for the old tracks," his Driver told him.

Edward was first to reach the house. **"I did it!"** he gasped when he stopped outside. **"I won!"**

Suddenly his pistons stopped aching and his axles stopped shaking. It was his happiest day. Now Edward knew what it felt like to be a Really Useful Engine. And he even has a new name – he's **Edward the Great!**

Read a story with Thomas

"Peep! Would you like to read Edward's story yourself? These pictures will help you. When you see the pictures, say the words."

A fast engine called  took the Duke and Duchess to their holiday house.

"He's a big show-off!" said .

 needed an engine to take their things.

"Send me please, Sir!" said .

"No, I'll do it!" said . "Let me go!"

They wanted to race .

But  chose slow old .

"Oh, no! Now  will win the race,"

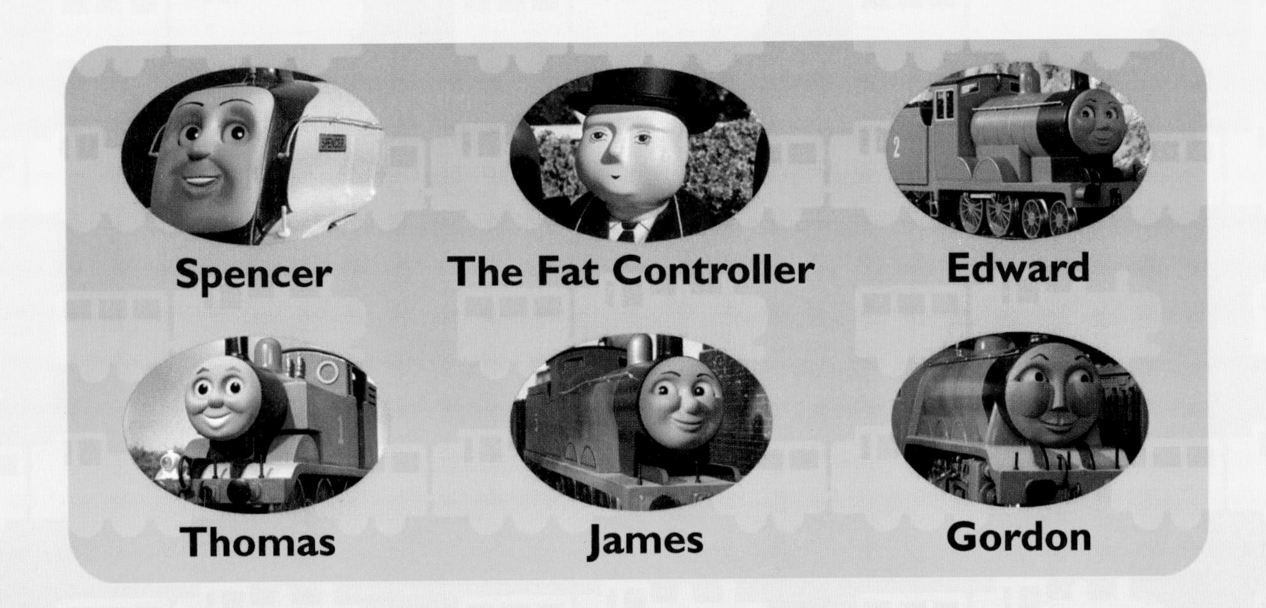

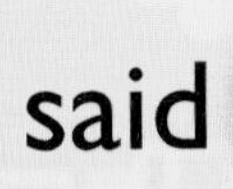
said  . "He's much faster."

 soon left  far behind.

"I've won the race already!" he said.

But when  fell asleep 

chuffed past him!

"Well done!" said  .

Slow old  won the race!

Now he's called  the Great!

Counting fun

"I need an engine to do three special jobs for me," said The Fat Controller one day.

Thomas was tired, but he wanted to help. "I'll go!" he said.

"Take the chickens to the market, the sheep to the farm and the children to the school, please, Thomas," said The Fat Controller.

But Thomas got mixed up! He took the sheep to the market.

He took the children to the farm.

He took the chickens to the school!

1. How many sheep did Thomas take to the market?

2. Thomas took the children to the farm. How many pigs did they see there?

3. How many chickens did Thomas take to the school?

ANSWERS: 1. seven sheep; 2. three pigs; 3. thirteen chickens.

Emily's new route

It was summer on the Island of Sodor and there was a lot of work for the engines to do, carrying passengers and goods up and down the lines.

But the engines like being busy, so they were happy.

All except Emily.

She was down at the Docks with Salty, shunting trucks into the sidings, and she didn't like the work at all.

Salty tried to cheer her up with one of his stories. "It's about a lighthouse, a box of oranges and a fishing rod," said Salty. "It all started when ..."

But only Salty seemed to know what his stories were about, and Emily soon stopped listening.

"Oh, I wish I could do something different," she said.

Emily's wish came true the very next morning!

"I am opening up some new routes," said The Fat Controller. "Emily, I want you to pull the special going to the flour mill."

Emily couldn't wait to tell James and Thomas about her new job.

"That's a good job, better than mine," said James. "I have to run to Black Loch. There are big stones on the track that bash my buffers and scratch my lovely red paint."

"And he's frightened of the Black Loch Monster," added Thomas.

"A monster? What's that?" asked Emily.

"Nobody really knows," said Thomas. "There are black things in the water, dark shapes that come and go."

"Nonsense!" said James. "It's just a story. At least, I think so ..."

But Emily wasn't so sure, and she was glad she didn't have to go to Black Loch.

The next morning, Emily puffed to the mill and the flour was loaded on to her trucks. Then she took the flour to the bakery.

But the trucks decided to be naughty.

"Hold back, hold back!" they screeched. They put their brakes on so that Emily had to pull really hard. It made her very slow and she was so late that there was no flour to make fresh bread that day.

The Fat Controller didn't have any toast for breakfast, and he was very cross. "If you're late again, I'll send you to Black Loch instead of James," he told her.

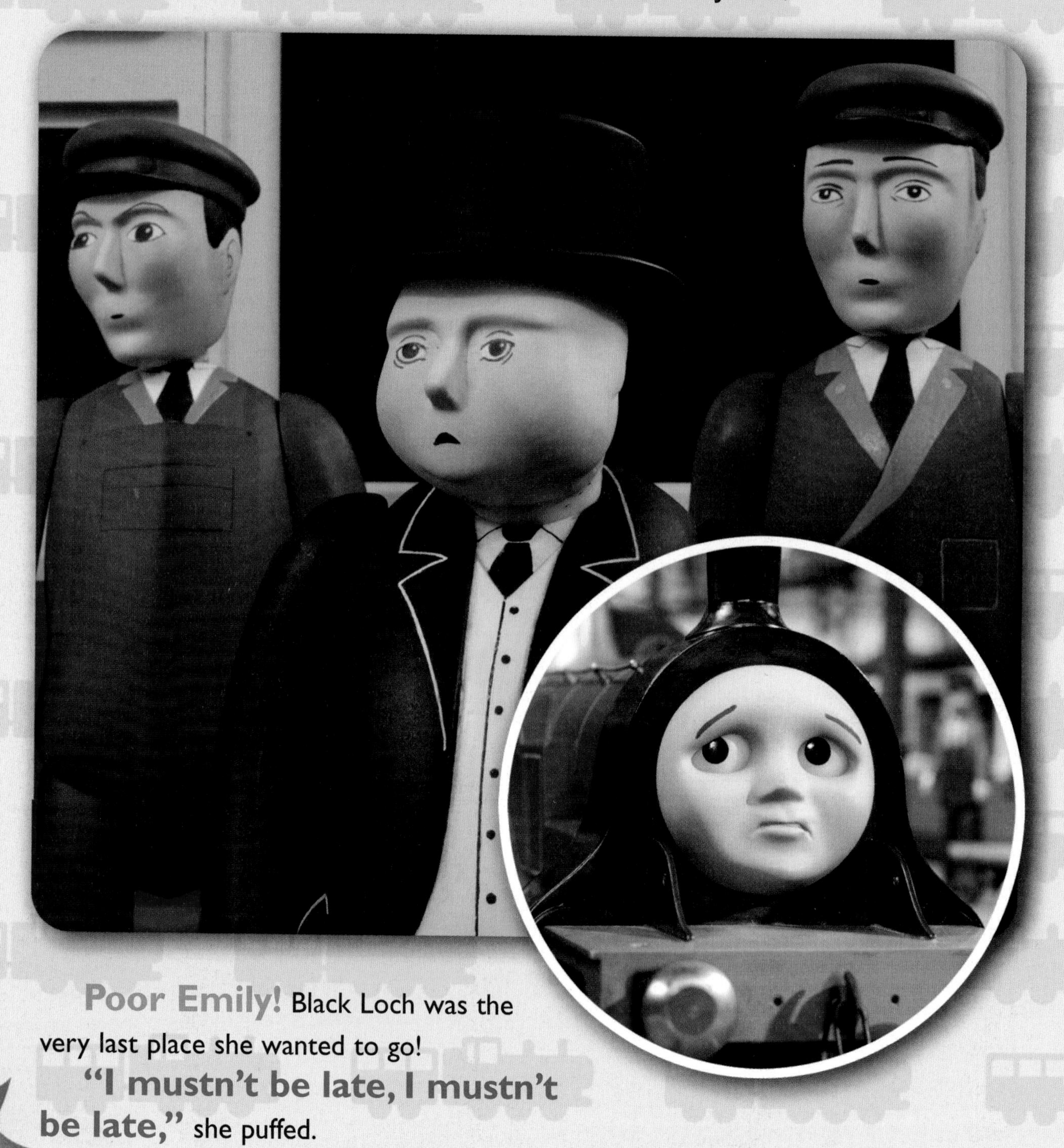

Poor Emily! Black Loch was the very last place she wanted to go!

"I mustn't be late, I mustn't be late," she puffed.

But the next morning the trucks were still playing tricks.

"Off we go, off we go!" they giggled. **"Mustn't be late, mustn't be late."**

But the trucks weren't coupled up properly and when Emily puffed away, she left some of them behind!

She had to go all the way back to get them.

But still the trucks were being naughty.

"Emily's late, Emily's late!" they sang.

That made Emily cross – **very** cross. She biffed the trucks so hard that they rolled into the duck pond with a big **SPLASH!** The flour went into the water and made a sticky, gooey white mess. The trucks were covered in it – **and so was Emily.**

Emily was in even more trouble now.

"I am not at all pleased with you," The Fat Controller told her. "You must do the Black Loch run instead of James."

"Oh, no," said Emily. **"Not Black Loch!"**

Thomas tried to make her feel better. "Wait and see," he said. "You might like the run, after all."

"What, bashed buffers, scratched paint and a big monster?" said Emily sadly. **"I don't think so!"**

The next morning Emily puffed to the station to collect her passengers. They were on holiday, and she could see that they were really looking forward to their trip.

Emily knew she mustn't let them down, so she took a big breath and steamed off.

Emily was puffing along beside Black Loch when rocks fell from the hillside and blocked the line.

She was waiting for help when the water in the loch **splashed** and **splished** and she saw dark shapes moving towards the shore.

Emily's boiler shivered and her valves rattled. She was very scared. **"It's the Monster!"** she cried.

But it wasn't a monster at all – it was a family of seals who had come to say hello!

"Onk, onk!" said the seals.

Emily liked the seals so much that after work that night she took Thomas to meet them.

"You were right, Thomas," said Emily. "I did like the Black Loch run, after all."

"Peep, peep!" said Thomas.

"Onk, onk!" said the seals.

Picture puzzles

These big pictures are from Emily's story. Look at them, then look at the little pictures under each one. Which of the little pictures you can see in the big ones? Write ✓ for yes or ✗ for no.

A

B

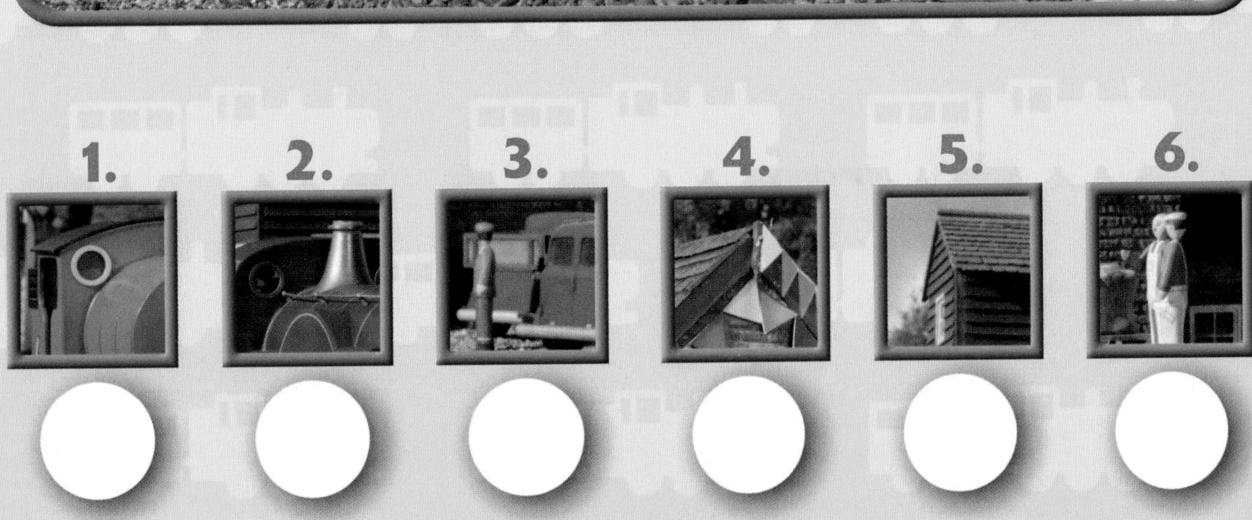

ANSWERS: A. pictures 1, 2 and 4; B. pictures 2, 3, 5 and 6.

Percy and the magic carpet

It was a very windy day on the Island of Sodor. Tree branches bent this way and that, and leaves flew all around. **WHOOSH!** At Maron Station, the wind blew The Fat Controller's top hat off!

But the engines didn't mind the windy weather. They were all looking forward to helping with the Sodor Flower Show.

At Tidmouth sheds, The Fat Controller had some news for the engines. "I need an engine to collect a special and get it to Maithwaite Station before Alicia Botti arrives. She's a famous singer and she's going to open the Flower Show."

All the engines wanted the job but The Fat Controller gave it to little Percy, the green Number 6 engine.

Percy was pleased, but Gordon wasn't.

"If the train was that special The Fat Controller would have sent me," he said. As he set off, Percy wondered what the special might be.

Percy found out when he arrived at the Docks, where Cranky the Crane was unloading the special.

"A roll of red carpet!" said Percy. **"What's so special about that?"**

"Maybe it's a **magic** carpet, matey!" said Salty. "I've heard stories about them. You say magic words like **abracadabra** and **shazam** and the carpet flies around in the air!"

"Well it doesn't look very magic to me," said Percy as Cranky lowered the carpet on to his flatbed.

Nobody noticed that Cranky's big hook got caught on the straps tied around the carpet.

As Percy puffed away, the straps snapped and the carpet started to unroll.

Soon the end was flapping about ...

When Percy stopped at a junction Gordon was waiting there, too. **"So your special is an old carpet!"** he roared. "No wonder The Fat Controller gave you the job!"

Just then, the wind blew so hard that the carpet flipped and flapped, then flew up into the air!

Percy was amazed. "Look!" he said. "It's not just any old carpet – **it's a magic carpet! It can fly!"**

When Murdoch passed by the wind blew the carpet up into the air again and it landed on one of his trucks.

"Oh, no!" said Percy. "My magic carpet is going off without me! **Come back!"**

He hurried after Murdoch. "Stop! Wait for me!" he wheeshed.

But Murdoch didn't hear him, ...

James was taking on passengers at Maron Station when Percy steamed through.

"Help me!" cried Percy. **"Murdoch has got my magic carpet!"**

"Silly little engine!" said James. "There's no such thing as a magic carpet."

Out in the countryside another gust of wind lifted the carpet off Murdoch's truck – and dropped it on Toby's roof!

"See, the carpet IS magic!" said Percy. **"It can fly!"**

He chased after Toby, but he didn't catch him until he stopped at Kellsthorpe Station, where Gordon was taking on water.

There, the wind lifted the carpet again and it slipped off Toby.

It landed on one of the tracks – **the track Thomas was steaming along at full speed!**

"We must warn Thomas!" cried Percy, and he and Gordon blew their whistles as loudly as they could.

"PEEP!" they blew. "PEEP, PEEP!"

Thomas heard the whistles and put on his brakes.

"He won't be able to stop in time!" said Percy. But then he remembered the magic words Salty had told him about.

"Abracadabra!" cried Percy. "Shazam!"

Nothing happened.

Percy decided to try another magic word. "Please?" he whispered.

Suddenly the wind blew again and the carpet flew up off the tracks and into the air. This time it landed on Percy's flatbed.

Thomas was safe!

Gordon gasped. "That carpet really is magic!" he said.

Later on, when Percy puffed into Maithwaite Station, The Fat Controller was waiting for him.

"Am I late?" asked Percy. "The magic carpet flew away and landed on Murdoch and then on Toby and I had to catch it and then ... "

The Fat Controller held up his hand and smiled. "No, you're not late, Percy. You're right on time, which means **you're a Really Useful Engine.**"

Little Percy felt very proud indeed.

The red carpet was laid out on the platform just before Gordon arrived with Alicia Botti.

After she had gone off to open the Flower Show, Percy and Gordon thought about the carpet. The Fat Controller had told them there was no such thing as a magic carpet. It was just a story.

But Gordon and Percy were not so sure ...

"Do you believe in magic, Gordon?" asked Percy.

Gordon just smiled ...

Calling all engines!

One day, The Fat Controller told Thomas and his friends that a new airport was going to be built on Sodor. The steam engines wanted to help with the work – but so did the diesels.

Do you think that Thomas persuaded the steamies and the diesels to work together instead of squabbling?

Can you point to Thomas and his friends and say their names?

ANSWERS: Engines from left to right are Edward, Henry, James, Thomas, Percy, Gordon and Emily.

These clues tell you about some of Thomas' friends. Find the right picture for each clue.

1

I am a shunting engine.
I like being sneaky.
My name begins with D.
Who am I?

2

I am a tram engine.
My coach is called Henrietta.
I am made of wood.
Who am I?

3

I am the oldest engine.
I am blue.
My number is 2.
Who am I?

4

I have dark green paint.
I have a tall shiny brass funnel.
My name begins with E.
Who am I?

ANSWERS: 1. Diesel; 2. Toby; 3. Edward; 4. Emily.

Read a story with Thomas

"Here's a story about Gordon you can read with me! The little pictures will help you. When you see the pictures in the story, say the words. The story's called **Squeak, rattle and knock** so make sure you make lots of **squeak, rattle, knock** and **peep** noises. I'm going to!"

One day, when  was pulling the

Express  was on the line.

He was cross when he had to back up.

"You steamies are no good!" said .

"You'll all be scrapped!"

"Pah!" said . "Not me!

I'm as fast as I ever was!" But later on

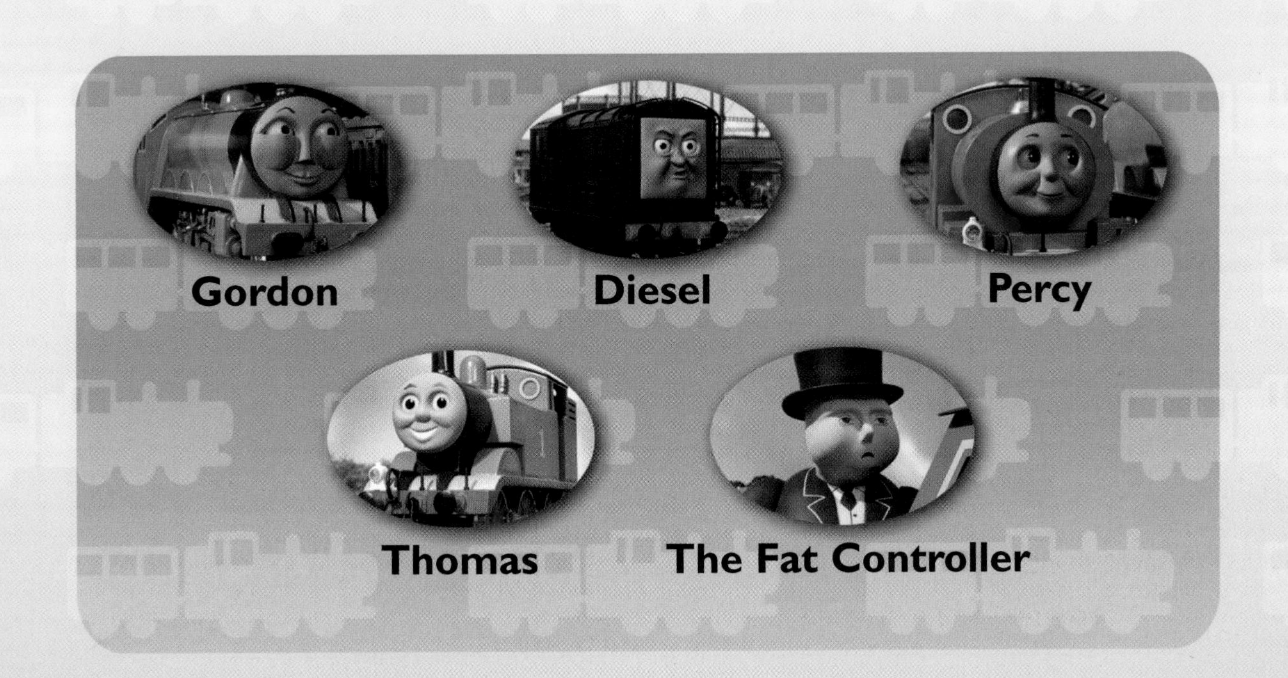

 made a noise: **SQUEAK!**

"Oh, no," he said. "I don't want to

be scrapped!"  blew his

whistle so no one could hear the

squeak, **PEEP! PEEP!** But when he went

up his hill,  had to slow down.

The slower he went, the quieter he was.

"Aha!" he said. "If I go slowly, no one will hear me squeak, not even  !"

The next day waited until  and 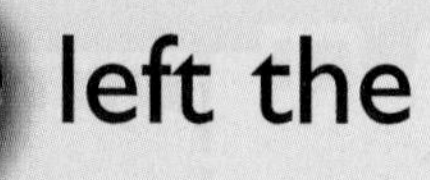 left the sheds then he rolled out very slowly.

But he made another noise, **RATTLE!**

"Oh, no," he said. "  was right!  will scrap me!" went so slowly that he made  cross.

"It won't do!" he said. "You must go faster!"

So 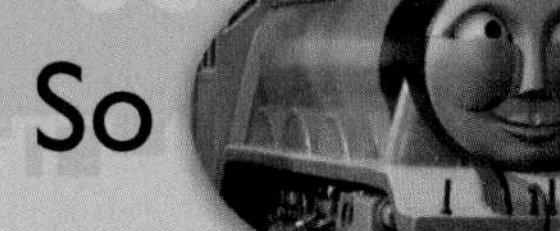 rushed to the Docks:

SQUEAK! RATTLE! then **KNOCK!**

"Well done, ," said .

"Now off you go to the repair yard."

 was surprised. "So you're not going to scrap me?" he said.

"My fastest engine?" said .

"Of course not!"

Soon  was as good as new.

Now he makes a happy noise, **PEEEP!**

Colouring fun

Colour in this picture of Toby the Tram Engine and his coach Henrietta then write your name on the line. They are both brown.

Toby and Henrietta

by ____________________

Donald and Douglas are from Scotland. They are twin engines so colour them both the same then write your name on the line.

Donald and Douglas

by ____________________

James goes too far

It was winter on Sodor. The engines had to work extra-hard to steam through the thick snow that lay on the tracks.

James was out in the countryside pulling the slow goods train, taking big wagons from one side of the Island to the other.

Some carried animal feed.

Some carried tar.

Some carried bricks.

James stopped at a red signal and Percy pulled up beside him. He was carrying the mail.

When the signal changed to green, Percy set off in a flash.

"Goodbye, James!" he whistled.

"Humph! It's not fair," grumbled James. **"I was here first. Why did the Signalman let Percy go first?"**

His Driver explained. "He has to let Percy through because he's pulling the mail train," he said. "Letters and parcels are more important than slow goods."

"Humph!" said James.

Later on when James stopped for water, Thomas rolled in front of him.

"You must let me go first," said Thomas. "I'm a guaranteed connection."

"It's not fair!" said James. "You engines all have more important jobs than me."

"Nonsense!" said Thomas. **"We all know you're a Really Useful Engine."**

But that was the problem. James didn't want to be just Really Useful. He wanted to be **important.**

James got his chance to be important the very next morning.

"You must take coal to all the stations for the waiting-room fires so the passengers will be warm," said The Fat Controller. **"It's a very important job."**

James was so proud and excited that he tingled from funnel to firebox.

"I've got an important job now," he told Gordon.

But Gordon just sniffed. "I don't know what's so important about a load of coal!"

James huffed over to the water tower. Thomas and Percy were waiting, but James didn't want to join the queue.

"Come on, make way!" he steamed. **"I have an important job to do!"**

But Thomas and Percy didn't move.

James felt too important to wait with the others – so he didn't. Instead of taking on water he rushed off to the coaling station.

James met Edward at a junction. "I've got such a lot to do," said Edward. "Can you take these flat trucks to the Quarry for me?"

"No I can't!" said James as the signal changed and he hurried off to the coaling station. "I've got a very important job of my own to do."

Later on, James set off with the coal trucks. He felt very pleased with himself. **"Now I'm important,"** he chuffed.

James went faster and faster.

But he had to puff harder and harder.

He felt hotter and hotter.

Then he had to stop.

"What's wrong with me?" asked James.

"There's no water in your tanks," said his Driver.

When Edward arrived James said, "Will you push me to the water tower?"

"Sorry, I can't," said Edward, steaming away. "You wouldn't take my trucks to the Quarry, so now **I'm late and I can't stop.** But I'll ask the Signalman to send Salty with some water for you."

"Why didn't you fill up with water, matey?" asked Salty.

"I'm too important to join a queue," said James.

"I heard you were too important to help Edward, too," said Salty.

"Well, I've got the most important job on the Island," said James.

"No job is more important than helping another engine," said Salty.

Deep down in his boiler, **James knew Salty was right ...**

He was on his way again when he saw Diesel, who had broken down. He didn't like Diesel, but when he remembered Salty's words he stopped to help him.

"I'll push you back to the sheds," said James.

But pushing Diesel as well as pulling coal trucks was hard work and by the time James set off to deliver the coal, the sky was dark and snow was falling.

That night, James steamed all over the Island delivering coal to the station waiting rooms. Thanks to him, the passengers all had somewhere warm to wait.

In the morning, The Fat Controller arrived to see him. He knew that James had run out of water and that he had refused to help Edward.

"I'm sorry I put my own job first," said James.

But The Fat Controller also knew about James pushing Diesel back to the sheds.

"You helped another engine," said The Fat Controller. "And you delivered the coal on time, too. **You are a Really Useful Engine, James."**

James was so proud that he almost burst his boiler. "Thank you, Sir," he said.

James had learned that being **Really Useful** was much better than being **important.**

1